GABBY'S DOLLHOUSE

THE SPARKLIEST DAY OF THE YEAR

ORCHARD BOOKS

First published in Great Britain in 2023 by Hodder & Stoughton

DreamWorks Gabby's Dollhouse © 2023 DreamWorks Animation LLC. All Rights Reserved

A CIP catalogue record for this book is available from the British Library

ISBN 978 1 40837 053 7

1 3 5 7 9 10 8 6 4 2

Printed and bound in China

Orchard Books
An imprint of Hachette Children's Group
part of Hodder & Stoughton Limited
Carmelite House
50 Victoria Embankment
London EC4Y 0DZ
An Hachette UK Company
www.hachette.co.uk
www.hachettechildrens.co.uk

This book belongs to:

_____

Gabby was in her room trying out new hairstyles when she heard some familiar musical meows. That sound could only mean one thing – it was time for a Dollhouse Delivery!

What could it be? Gabby wondered. She opened the Meow Meow Mailbox and took out a pretty box. It had sparkly ears and looked a bit like MerCat.

Inside the box, she found a flask and two tiny tubes filled with colourful liquid.

"I think I'm supposed to mix them," said Gabby, studying the directions.

First, she put on her safety glasses, then she carefully poured the contents of both tubes into the flask. The yellow and blue combined to make green. The green potion began to sparkle, and then . . . POOF!

Suddenly, Gabby was wearing a pink fluffy bathrobe. There was something in the pocket – an invitation to MerCat's Spa Day Party in the dollhouse!

"It's time to get tiny!" said Gabby. With a little magic, Gabby and Pandy Paws shrank and found themselves inside the dollhouse.

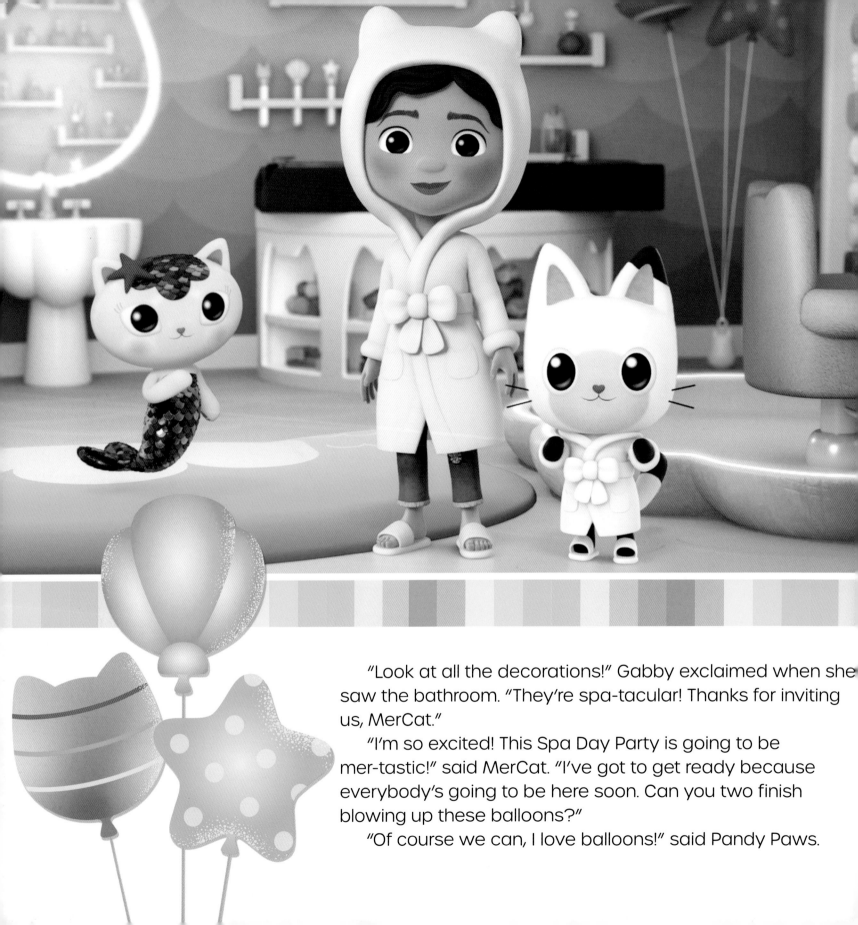

"Look at all the decorations!" Gabby exclaimed when she saw the bathroom. "They're spa-tacular! Thanks for inviting us, MerCat."

"I'm so excited! This Spa Day Party is going to be mer-tastic!" said MerCat. "I've got to get ready because everybody's going to be here soon. Can you two finish blowing up these balloons?"

"Of course we can, I love balloons!" said Pandy Paws.

Pandy Paws got to work, but his balloon got away from him. It flew around the room, knocking over a potion bottle that spilled right on to MerCat!

"I'm fine!" said MerCat, but she didn't look quite right. Her colour and sparkle were starting to disappear.

"Oh, no!" said MerCat, looking at the bottle. "This is my Magical Spot Removing Potion. It's for stains but it seems to be making my sparkle fade!"

"I'm so sorry," said Pandy Paws, sadly.

"It's OK, Pandy. It was just an accident," said MerCat.

"But today is your Spa Day Party," said Pandy Paws. "It's the sparkliest, shiniest day of the whole year!"

"That's true," said MerCat, looking worried.

"Don't worry, MerCat. We're going to get your sparkle back in time for the party!" Gabby said.

"But how?" asked MerCat.

"I don't know yet. Let me think . . . " Gabby said, her mind whirling.

"Wait! Isn't Cakey Cat making face masks for the party? Maybe they will help you get your sparkle back!" suggested Pandy Paws.

"It's worth a try," said MerCat.

"To the kitchen!" shouted Pandy Paws.

Cakey was in the kitchen getting ready for the party.

"MerCat! Your sparkle's gone!" gasped Cakey.

"That's why we're here," said MerCat.

"We're hoping your face masks will help MerCat get her colour and sparkle back," Gabby explained.

"Yes! My face masks always do the trick!" said Cakey Cat.

"Today, we're making my Squishy Squeezy Glow Masks," said Cakey. "We need avocado, lemon and honey."

"What should we do first, Cakey?" Gabby asked.

"Scoop out the avocado with a spoon," explained Cakey. "Now for the fun part! Use your hands to mash up the avocado. Squeeze in a dash of lemon and a drop of honey. Then mash it up again! Now it's ready!"

Cakey showed everyone how to put on the Squishy Squeezy Glow Masks. Pandy Paws, MerCat and Gabby patted the green mixture on to their faces.

"I hope this works," said MerCat, nervously.

"There's only one way to find out!" said Cakey.

"Let's see the results," said Cakey.

MerCat wiped away her face mask. "Oh, shimmering sea scales! It worked!" she said. "Now, I just have to get the rest of my sparkle back."

"Well, Baby Box and Mama Box are making soap for the party. Maybe that could help," Gabby suggested.

"To the craft room!" shouted Pandy Paws.

"Hey, Gabby. Hey, Pandy. MerCat, what happened?" asked Baby Box in the craft room.

"I spilled a potion and she lost her sparkle . . . on Spa Day, the sparkliest, shiniest day of the year!" Pandy Paws replied.

"Don't worry, MerCat. We can help," Mama Box reassured her.

"I know! We can make our super soaps," said Baby Box. "Let's get crafting!"

After choosing different colours, Mama Box melted the soap.

"What shape do you want your soap to be?" Baby Box asked them.

"The heart shape, please!" Gabby said.

Pandy Paws, MerCat and Baby Box chose their shapes, too.

"Now we get to pick a super special charm to add to our soaps," said Baby Box. "The charms are what make the super soap super!"

Everyone added a special charm, then Mama Box put the soaps in the refrigerator to set.

"The soaps are ready!"
announced Mama Box.
"Check out my delicious pickle
ice lolly!" said Pandy Paws.

"MerCat, your super
soap looks just like you!"
Gabby said.
"Are you ready to give
it a try?" asked Pandy
Paws.

"OK, super soap, I'm counting on you!" said MerCat. She started to scrub. "It's working!"

"Your colour is coming back!" Gabby exclaimed.

Everyone cheered.

"Yuck!" said a voice, interrupting the cheers. "What's wrong with this ice lolly? It tastes terrible!"

"CatRat! It's not a real ice lolly, it's soap!" said Pandy Paws.

"That's silly! Who makes an ice lolly out of soap? Anyway, I'll see you at the party!" said CatRat.

"Oh no! It's almost time for the spa party and I still don't have my sparkle tail back," said MerCat. "But I have an idea. All mermaid cats keep one extra magical scale in a secret spot. If we can get the scale, I can use it to help me get my sparkle tail back! To the bathroom!"

"My scale is with all the other magical mermaid scales deep in the sea in Mermaidlantis, but there's a way we can bring it to us. If we play the secret colour code on this shell chime, the scale will come up to us," MerCat explained.

"Great!" Gabby said. "Give me the code and I'll play it!"

"The spinner will give us the code. We just need to remember the colours and play them in the right order," said MerCat.

"How are we going to remember them all?" asked Pandy Paws.

"I have an idea for that!" said Gabby. She asked MerCat to paint her fingernails to match the colours in the code.

"Now we have the code right at my fingertips," Gabby said with a laugh.

Pandy Paws followed the colour code on Gabby's nails and played each chime in order: pink, blue, green, yellow, orange. WHOOSH! Arthur came up from Mermaidlantis with MerCat's scale!

"Hopefully this will bring my sparkle tail back!" MerCat said excitedly. She dropped it in the bath and jumped in just as the rest of her guests arrived.

"Where's MerCat?" asked Baby Box.

"Right here," said MerCat, peeking out of the tub.

"Did it work?" Gabby asked her.

"Did you get your sparkle back?" said Baby Box.

"Guess there's only one way to find out. Fins crossed," MerCat said. She leapt out of the bath with a splash. "It's back! Thank you, everyone. It just wouldn't be a Spa Day without my sparkle tail!"

"Let's get this party started," said MerCat. "Hit it, Catnip!"
DJ Catnip started spinning some tunes.

While Mama Box got some rest and relaxation, Baby Box painted her nails in her favourite colours.

CatRat enjoyed a sweet smoothie and one of Cakey Cat's Squishy Squeezy Glow Masks.

Pandy Paws took a luxurious bubble bath.

And Gabby finally got a perfect new hairstyle!
"Oh, MerCat, I love it! It's so sparkly!" Gabby exclaimed.
"Of course it is! This is Spa Day Party – the sparkliest day of the year!" MerCat replied with a smile.

Are you ready for a surprise?
You get to pick the Gabby Cat of the Day!
Chose your favourite Gabby Cat and make up a song for them.